ROB CHILDS

THE BIG BREAK

Illustrated by Aidan Potts

YOUNG CORGI BOOKS

THE BIG BREAK
A YOUNG CORGI BOOK : 0 552 529664

First Publication in Great Britain

PRINTING HISTORY
Young Corgi edition published 1997
Reprinted 1998

Set in 14/18pt Linotype New Century Schoolbook by
Phoenix Typesetting, Ilkley, West Yorkshire.

Young Corgi Books are published by Transworld Publishers Ltd,
61–63 Uxbridge Road, Ealing, London W5 5SA,
in Australia by Transworld Publishers (Australia) Pty Ltd,
15–25 Helles Avenue, Moorebank, NSW 2170,
and in New Zealand by Transworld Publishers (NZ) Ltd,
3 William Pickering Drive, Albany, Auckland.

Made and printed in Great Britain by
Mackays of Chatham PLC, Chatham, Kent

With thanks to Gina Pollinger
for my own big break as a writer

1 What's Your Name?

'Great to be back!' cried Andrew Weston, pointing up at one of the hostel's second-floor windows. 'That's the room we slept in last time.'

'Don't remember getting much sleep,' grinned Tim. 'We were too busy raiding the *Demons'* dormitory!'

'We'll have some fun tonight, too,' Andrew laughed. 'I've brought an Easter Egg for a midnight feast.'

Mr Lawrence lifted the boys' suitcases out of the car boot. 'See you on

Friday, Dad,' said Tim, hiding any nerves with a smile.

'Thanks again for bringing us, Mr Lawrence,' Andrew called out as he lugged his case and sports bag towards the entrance to the hostel.

'Good luck, both of you. Show United's coaches what you can do!'

Four fabulous days of football lay ahead, the reward for their excellent performances in a New Year five-a-

side Festival. United's talent scouts had picked out a number of lads from the tournament for this Easter coaching course and Andrew recognized two of them across the crowded foyer. But he was keeping an eye out for one player in particular.

'No sign of Dean yet,' he hissed to Tim as they checked in at the reception desk. 'I'm sure he was offered a place on the course.'

'Not to worry, you won't be able to miss a head his size for long!'

Andrew's team, the *Vikings*, had clashed with *Dean's Demons* more than once over that New Year weekend, on and off the pitch. He guessed that Dean would probably try to make some trouble again, but never expected to find themselves actually sharing the same dormitory.

'Well, look who it isn't!' came the

sarcastic greeting as Andrew pushed open the door. 'You two are gonna get shown up real bad this week.'

'Nice to see you again, too, Dean!' Tim replied likewise, swinging his bag up onto a top bunk to claim it before Andrew. 'You haven't changed.'

'No, he's still wearing the same socks, judging by the smell in here,' gasped Andrew. 'Somebody open the windows, quick.'

A gong sounded before any argument could develop. 'Time for lunch,' announced a voice from a lower bunk behind Dean. As the boy stood up, they saw it was the *Demons*' goalkeeper.

'Any more of you lot?' Tim asked.

'Just us two stars,' Dean smirked. 'C'mon, Scott, let's go down and grab some grub. We don't want to have to sit with these no-hopers.'

When they'd gone, Andrew pulled his red *Vikings* shirt out of his bag and displayed the large white V on the front. 'I've decided to wear this today just to annoy Dean,' he grinned.

The first coaching session began in mid-afternoon on United's vast training ground. As the youngsters gazed around in wonder, one of the club's top players was seen jogging along in the distance on his own.

'Hey! That's Jeff Robson, isn't it?'

cried Andrew. 'He's been out of the team with a knee injury. Hope I can get his autograph later.'

'You'll be lucky! Bet he won't come anywhere near us.'

Tim was wrong. As the coaches led them through a series of warming-up exercises, the England international paused nearby for a breather. 'Any talent here, Kev?' he called out.

'Doubt it,' United's youth coach grinned. 'Twelve years of age and they're bending and stretching like a bunch of old men!'

Kev sent the boys off with a football each into an area marked out with square grids. 'We want to see you dribbling a ball about,' he said. 'Keep on the move, twisting and turning, but make no contact with anyone else.'

The individual players were quickly lost in a whirl of swaying bodies,

sporting a dazzling array of coloured kits. Each one was hoping to catch the eye as well with some well-practised piece of fancy footwork.

Nobody wanted to be seen losing control of the ball, however, and they were extra careful when their mazy paths took them close to where Robson was standing. Andrew especially. As a hard-tackling defender, he wasn't picked in his school team for his dribbling skills, and he had to focus all his attention on the ball. He didn't even see Dean coming.

As Dean zipped past, he suddenly kicked out and sent Andrew's ball bouncing away out of the grids. Andrew yelled a complaint, but it was no use. Dean was gone. Red-faced, Andrew trotted after the stray ball, only to find it trapped under Robson's foot.

'Never mind, son,' the international grinned. 'Happens to the best of us. Come on, try and get it back off me.'

Andrew could scarcely believe his ears. Here he was, in the first few minutes, being invited to challenge one of his favourite players for the ball. He closed up hesitantly, not quite knowing how serious Robson was.

The player toyed with the ball, offering a chance for the boy to nip it away. But as Andrew made a move, Robson dragged it back out of reach with the sole of his expensive trainer. Andrew had another stab at it, but once more the ball disappeared, shielded cleverly now by his legs and body.

Andrew glanced back round and was amazed to see that everyone had stopped to watch this little duel. He caught sight of Dean's mocking face.

'Right, I'm not going to let Robson

make a monkey out of me in front of Dean,' Andrew decided. 'If he wants me to get it, I'll get it!'

He harrassed Robson with more determination, but was still unable to win the ball. 'Good, don't give up, keep tight on me,' the star urged.

Robson lost concentration for a moment with speaking and Andrew pounced. He lunged in firmly, wrapping the side of his foot round the ball to block it. The unexpected force of his tackle made Robson lose his balance, slip and finish up sitting on the grass – without the ball.

'Foul, ref!' he laughed. 'He took the man first.'

The coaches enjoyed his discomfort hugely, seeing Robson upended like that. 'No foul!' Kev yelled. 'The kid won the ball cleanly. Serves you right for trying to show off!'

'Er, s . . . sorry, Jeff . . . Mr Robson,' Andrew stammered, realizing the damage he might have done. 'Is your knee OK?'

'No need to apologize, I'm fine,' he replied. 'Just help me up, will you? What's your name?'

'Andrew – Andrew Weston.'

'Right, Andy, I'll remember you. If we ever meet in a league game one day, I'll know to stay well away from your tackles!'

Andrew rejoined the others in a daze as Kev organized groups for passing practice. 'Don't be shy with each other,' the coach told them. 'If you don't know somebody's name, just ask him.'

Kev did exactly that himself. He picked out the tall, dark-haired lad with the big white letter V on his shirt and sidled over for a quiet word.

'Andrew, isn't it?' he began. 'Well done, you've soon made your mark on Jeff Robson – and everybody else. We all know *your* name now!'

2 Greedy!

The first day's session ended with a series of four-a-side games.

'No goalies, nobody can handle the ball,' Kev stressed. 'Take kick-ins when it goes out of play.'

Andrew wasn't too surprised when fate paired Tim and himself with Dean and Scott. 'Makes a change to be on the same side,' he remarked.

Dean sneered. 'The only things we've got in common are these blue bibs. Don't expect any help from me.'

'I wasn't counting on it,' Andrew retorted.

Their foursome did not demonstrate the greatest of teamwork. Dean had no intention of passing to either Tim or Andrew, and Scott was sulking over the no-keeper rule.

'When do I get a chance to show my skills in goal?' he moaned.

Kev's assistant coach, Eddie, overheard him. 'You'd rather go back home, boy?' he said icily.

'No, it's just that . . .'

'Right, then, quit belly-aching. There's plenty of time this week for us to admire your wonderful goalkeeping!'

'Not a good start, pal. That's you in their black books already,' Dean teased him, following his jibe up with an awkward pass to Scott who was easily robbed by an opponent.

The boy stroked the ball accurately

towards the narrow coned target. It looked a certain goal until Andrew scampered back, just managing to stretch out a leg to deflect the shot wide. The resulting corner was a poor one. Tim chested the ball down, clipped it out to Dean and then ran forward willingly in support. He was wasting his energy.

No way was Dean going to give him the ball back. The big striker held on

to it himself, trying to burst past a defender by sheer force, but the other player was equally determined. He timed his tackle well, winning possession from Dean and setting up an attack of their own. This one ended in success with the ball tucked neatly between the unguarded cones.

'Greedy, Dean!' Kev shouted. 'Cost your side a goal, that did. Let's see you pass the ball a bit more to your team-mates.'

'Huh! Team*mates*, he calls them,' Dean scoffed. 'No chance!'

Dean did score a goal soon afterwards, a typically selfish, solo effort, but their opponents were never in any danger of defeat. They linked up with each other well, swapping swift passes, and they were 7-2 ahead when Kev whistled everyone to a halt.

At least that's what they claimed the score was. Andrew had stopped counting in disgust after the fourth goal went in. He and Tim fared somewhat better when they teamed up with different pairs in further short games, but Dean's attitude still rankled with them.

'It's a pity Dean acts like he does,' Andrew observed. 'He'd be a good player to have in your side, if he wasn't so pig-headed.'

'Right,' Tim nodded. 'We all know he can score goals. Just wish he'd let his feet do more of the talking and give his big mouth a rest!'

The coaches outlined their plans for the days ahead. 'Football – and then more football!' Eddie summed up with a grin. 'Plus orienteering on Thursday afternoon to help you get even fitter for football!'

'Under the showers now,' Kev ordered. 'The hostel doesn't want a load of dirty, sweaty players piling into their dining room for tea.'

Two dozen lads stripped off rather reluctantly in the changing rooms before braving the jets of hissing, steaming water.

'Ow! It's red-hot!' gasped Andrew as he took the plunge. 'If we're going to have this torture every day, we'll have no skin left by Friday.'

'More washes than you have all season!' Tim joked. 'You'll be so clean, your grandad won't recognize you when he comes to pick us up.'

As they paddled out of the showers and groped for their towels on a hand rail, Dean flicked out at them with the end of his own wet towel. He caught Tim painfully on the arm.

'Hey! Watch it!' Tim complained. 'That hurt.'

'It was meant to,' Dean laughed. 'What yer gonna do, tell tales on me to Kev? Or to Mummy when you get home?'

Tim turned his back on him and felt the stinging towel across his bare buttocks. He whirled round angrily, and both he and Andrew made a lunge towards Dean just as Eddie strode into the room.

'Hello, still got some energy to burn off, have we?' he began. 'Better save it for the orienteering. Now quit messing about and get dressed.'

'What exactly is this orienteering?' one of the players asked.

'Cross-country with map and compass,' Eddie replied. 'You lot will be racing through the woods, trying to work out where you are and where you're supposed to be going next. We'll see who's got brains as well as brawn!'

'What if we get lost?' came a somewhat anxious question.

The coach grinned mischievously. 'Then you won't get back to the hostel in time for tea that day!'

The hostel tuckshop did good business after the evening meal. The footballers had worked up a healthy appetite and were stocking up for their first night in the dormitories.

'Save your money, Tim. We've got my

Easter Egg to share later, remember,' said Andrew, leading the way into the games room.

They hardly saw Dean and Scott, apart from spotting them slumped in front of the television watching a video. By the time Andrew and Tim were finally persuaded up to their dormitory by the hostel manager, they found the two ex-Demons already lying in their bunks.

'You're a bit early,' said Andrew. 'Tired little boys, are you?'

'Yeah, tired of you two creeps,' Dean drawled, turning over the page of his soccer magazine.

'Video was dead boring too,' added Scott. 'Seen it before.'

Andrew shrugged, not bothering to respond. He still had some unpacking to do. He dragged his suitcase across the lower bunk towards him and found it was half-open. 'Funny!' he murmured. 'Positive I'd zipped it up properly before tea.'

When he opened the lid fully, he cried out in dismay. 'Hey! My egg's gone. I had a big Easter Egg in my case.'

Tim peered over the edge of his top bunk. 'Are you sure it was in there? You might have left it at home by mistake.'

'Course I'm sure. I put it in there myself this morning.'

Instinctively, Andrew whirled round to accuse Dean. 'Have you nicked my Easter Egg?'

'Who, me? Are you talking to me?' he demanded menacingly. 'What d'yer think I am?'

'I *know* what you are!' Andrew stated. 'You've even got some chocolate round your mouth. I can see it.'

'I gave him that,' Scott cut in. 'I

bought some bars of chocolate at the tuckshop.'

'I don't believe either of you,' said Andrew furiously, but Tim held him by the arm to stop his friend's temper getting the better of him.

'Don't go getting involved in a fight in here,' Tim warned him. 'The manager will report us to the coaches and we'd be sent home, I bet.'

Andrew unclenched his fists and tried to calm down. 'I know it was you,' he said, staring hard at Dean. 'Nobody else in this dorm would do anything like that.'

Dean returned his attention to the magazine. 'Prove it!' he said with a smirk.

3 Soccer Skills

'Your brother ought to be here for this,' Tim said, rolling the ball out to Andrew. 'I'm not much good in goal.'

'I've noticed,' Andrew grinned. 'Even our Chris would have scored!'

'You wait till it's your turn.'

Andrew's job at present was to act as feeder, passing the ball into the path of the player running in to strike at goal. They had spent the first part of the morning coaching session improving their heading ability and

now it was intensive shooting practice.

'Hit it first time,' growled Eddie as the next player needed two touches to control the ball before poking a tame shot straight at Tim. 'Keeper could have finished his breakfast while you were fiddling about.'

'But I'm a defender, Eddie,' the boy protested half-heartedly. 'The only goals I normally score are own ones!'

'You're too young to decide what you are,' the coach stated. 'You should try out different positions to see which suits you best.'

'What's the point?' Scott butted in rudely. 'I only want to play in goal.'

'Sounds just like our kid,' Andrew said to Tim out of the corner of his mouth. 'Chris has always got to be goalie.'

Eddie stared hard at Scott before

answering. 'The point is, sonny, it helps you to be more aware of other players' problems. Might even make you a better keeper in the end, knowing what attackers are trying to do.'

Scott shrugged. 'Maybe, but I thought I'd been picked to come here as a keeper. You haven't even seen me handle the ball yet.'

'OK, anything to shut you up,' he sighed. 'Let him have a go, Tim.'

Tim was out of goal even faster than Scott dashed into it, not giving the coach a chance to change his mind. Tim ran to take his place among the queue of shooters while Eddie took over Andrew's duties as feeder.

'I've already seen how you can tackle, Andy,' he grinned, 'so let's take a look at your marksmanship.'

Andrew was about to say he was a

defender, too, but bit his lip. Besides, there was nothing he liked better than joining the attack at times to get in a shot or header at goal himself.

Scott was determined to show Eddie what he could do between the posts. He saved the first two shots comfortably, saw the next sail wide, and then dived to his left to turn Tim's low drive round the foot of the post.

'Well done!' the coach said generously and tapped another ball forwards for Andrew to try his luck.

Andrew steadied himself as he ran in, but got his foot too much under the ball and ballooned it over the crossbar. It even went over the high wire fencing behind the goal.

'Ball bobbled up,' he said, making a lame excuse.

'Go and fetch,' Eddie laughed. 'Dribble it all the way back.'

Although Andrew had to put up with Scott's gloating cackle, he was glad at least to be spared Dean's ridicule. As he collected the ball, he watched Dean billow the netting in another practice group, and glanced back just in time to see Tim beat Scott for both pace and placement.

'Good shot!' Eddie praised him. 'Would have got past United's keeper, that one, I reckon.'

That was scant consolation for Scott. He scowled at Tim, but had no chance to make any snide remark. Already the next player was moving in and fired his shot to the goalkeeper's right.

Scott attempted to make the save look more spectacular than it needed to be. He dropped on to the ball deliberately late, but it slithered underneath his body and over the line. Eddie was not impressed.

'Why dive? Your granny could have bent down and picked that one up!'

Scott was rattled. He fumbled other shots, twice letting the ball run loose, mistakes that in a match might have been punished by goals from the rebounds. Perhaps his worst moment came when Andrew managed to slip one past him. Andrew's usual shooting method was to hit-and-hope, but this time he calmly sidefooted the ball and sneaked it in off a post.

Scott did not enjoy his packed lunch. He sat by himself moodily, dozed off in the dark while the rest watched a film on dribbling skills, and made little effort to put the techniques into practice afterwards.

His interest only perked up again when coloured bibs were handed out for six-a-side games – with goal-keepers. Eddie felt tempted to make Scott play out on the field, but pitted him against Dean instead.

'Magic!' Andrew smiled secretly, finding himself playing opposite Dean too. 'Been looking forward to this.'

So, it seemed, had Dean. He wasted no time in making his powerful presence felt, going in extra hard on Andrew, but the defender was waiting for it and steeled himself to resist the crude challenge.

'Midges must be biting early this year,' Andrew taunted him, sweeping his clearance out to the wing.

'Huh! It'll be alligators snapping at yer legs next time!' he sneered.

The striker soon demonstrated his goalscoring ability, however. For once, he managed to slip Andrew's shackles, beat a second defender and then lashed the ball towards goal. Scott barely saw it. The goalkeeper only stopped the ball as it came bouncing back out from the net.

Sadly, Dean continued to show the darker side of his character, too, throwing his weight around care-lessly. A wild elbow caught one opponent in the face, and when he went over the top of the ball to clatter another, Eddie stopped the game to wag his finger at him.

'If you'd been wearing studs and not

trainers, you could have done that lad some serious damage.'

Andrew wanted to make the point more forcibly. He bided his time until the right opportunity came along, which did so when Dean broke clear down the left. Andrew set his sights on his prey and knew that if he mistimed his tackle, Dean would either be through to score or badly fouled.

He made contact with bone-juddering force, making absolutely sure that his right foot took the ball away first before Dean felt the crunching impact. The striker was bowled over, winded, but soon hauled himself back onto his feet to seek revenge.

'Dirty fouler!' Dean howled. 'I'll get you for that.'

'Fair challenge, play on,' ordered Eddie firmly.

Dean tore off his green bib and threw

it down on the pitch in disgust, a tantrum that the coach would not tolerate. 'Off!' he bellowed. 'Come over here and sit on the grass until you're ready to apologize.'

'Wicked tackle, Andy!' grinned one of his teammates. 'Now I know why they call these things bibs – they're for big cry-babies like Dean!'

Kev, meanwhile, had been watching Tim enjoy himself in the other game, scoring two goals and making three more. As all the lads trailed back to the changing room afterwards for hot showers, the coaches compared notes.

The names of Tim, Andrew and Dean cropped up several times in their brief conversation, but for very different reasons . . .

4 In and Out

Thursday morning was spent indoors. Not only did the boys have the treat of watching United's first-team squad training in the gym, but they were also going to use it themselves afterwards.

As soon as they entered the gym, Jeff Robson began rubbing his injured knee. 'Watch it, men!' he cried, pointing Andrew out. 'This is the kid I was telling you about. Don't let him tackle you, whatever you do!'

The joke helped the boys overcome their shyness and many of them began to hold out pieces of paper and pens. 'Please can I have your autograph, Mr Robson?' Andrew asked politely, ignoring Dean's giggles behind him.

'Sure thing, Andy,' he grinned. 'Reckon you've deserved it.'

The other United players took the chance for a breather to mingle and chat with the youngsters, signing autographs freely. 'Wait till our kid hears about this,' Andrew laughed. 'Chris will be bright green with envy.'

'He probably won't believe you,' Tim replied.

Andrew waved his paper crammed with famous names. 'I've got proof!'

Dean was trying to act cool, leaning casually against the gym wall. *'Please can I have your autograph, Mr Robson?'* he mimicked Andrew.

Andrew shrugged off the taunt. 'It's not every day you get the chance to meet all these star players.'

Dean pulled a face. 'Who wants the autographs of these guys, anyway? County are my team, they're the best.'

'What are you doing here, then?' asked Tim. 'Don't you want to be picked to be coached at United's Centre of Excellence?'

'No way!' Dean scoffed. 'I'd turn it

down, if they offered me a place. Already got County's scouts begging me to go to their Centre.'

Tim tugged Andrew away. 'Ignore him, he's all mouth. Let's just hope that *we* both still stand a chance of being invited back here.'

'Up to us to make sure we are,' said Andrew with a gleam in his eye.

When United's players went outside to continue their own training, the two coaches worked the boys hard on basic ball skills. 'Quicker!' urged Eddie loudly. 'Pass and move, pass and move. C'mon, keep it going.'

Kev was quieter, but just as demanding in what he wanted them to try and do. 'One touch control, look up and pass. That's the way, well done!'

The session developed into a number of hectic, four-a-side contests. They were only allowed two touches when the ball came their way, one to control it and one to pass or shoot at the small unguarded goals.

'Free kick! You had three touches there, Dean,' shouted Eddie.

Kev went up to the scowling striker. 'Have to think a bit quicker at times. A good swift pass to a teammate in space is often better than holding the ball too long and letting people get marked up.'

'I'm a goalscorer,' he answered back boldly. 'They're supposed to pass to *me*, not the other way round.'

Kev glared at him. 'You may well be a promising young player, Dean, but you still have an awful lot to learn. And if you're not prepared to listen, you've got no future in this game. Certainly not here.'

'Fine by me,' Dean muttered under his breath as the coach walked away. 'I'm too good for this club anyway!'

'Hope you've all got some breath left for this afternoon's orienteering,' Kev said as the hungry footballers attacked their packed lunches on the grass near the gym. 'Because you're sure going to need it!'

As they munched happily away, enjoying the spring sunshine, the coaches instructed them in the *do's* and *don't's* of orienteering, especially about safety. 'If the worst comes to the worst and you're in serious trouble,' Eddie finished off, 'blow hard on your whistle – like this.'

He shattered the peace of the training ground with six long blasts and then grinned. 'If we hear that signal, we'll come a-running to find you!'

After a crash course in the use of a compass, the boys were taken in minibuses to dense woodland ten miles from the city. They drove deep into its heart along a rutted track until Kev and Eddie parked in a clearing.

'Don't worry if you're not too good with the compass yet,' Kev said as they studied their large-scale maps. 'This is orienteering for beginners. You can find your way about just using your maps and your brains!'

'Brains!' Tim said, affecting a groan. 'Why did I have to get lumbered with Andrew as my partner?'

Andrew pulled Tim's hood right over his head. 'OK, pal, just remember that when you get us lost, I've got the whistle to blow for help!'

'There are red and white marker flags at every checkpoint shown on your maps,' Eddie explained. 'Decide which route to take to reach each one and then try and get there as fast as you can to record its number.'

'Right, you've got two hours to find as many markers as possible,' Kev said as they checked their watches. 'Off you go when you're ready.'

'Good luck,' Eddie called out. 'May the best pair win.'

'Yeah, and that'll be us,' Dean boasted to his partner Scott. 'Piece of

cake. I've done this sort of thing before,
so just follow me, OK?'

He hurried off into the woods along a
bumpy trail, with Scott tagging along
behind, still trying to make sense of
his map. 'Which way are we going?'
Scott wailed.

'The quickest way,' Dean yelled
back. 'We're gonna take a few short
cuts. C'mon, let's nip across here
through the undergrowth.'

'Kev said we should keep to the paths.'

'Paths are for cissies,' Dean snapped. 'Do you want to find more markers than anybody else or not?'

Dean didn't wait for an answer. He charged on ahead, glancing to his right to see Andrew and Tim on a nearby track, having started from the clearing at a different point.

'Got time for a spot of sabotage, I reckon!' Dean sniggered to himself.

He found the first flag hanging on the branch of a tree and ripped it off so that Scott could write its number on their record sheet.

'You're not supposed to do that, are you?' said Scott, confused.

'No – nor this!' Dean grinned as he flung it away into the undergrowth. 'Just making life a bit more difficult

for our rivals. Nobody else will find that one now.'

They escaped only just in time as Tim and Andrew arrived on the scene less than a minute later. 'Are you sure this is the right place?' panted Andrew as they gazed about, trying to locate the flag.

'No, but I think so.'

'Let's just take a look at the map again.'

They sat down on a fallen tree trunk and compared a few features on the map with what they could see around them. 'There's the ruined wall,' Tim pointed out. 'And the stream running next to it. The flag ought to be just to the west a bit.'

'Which way's west?' asked Andrew, peering down at the compass.

'To the left.'

'Oh, right.'

'No, I said left. You must have your map the wrong way round. Orientate it properly.'

'I have. Keep turning the map the way you're facing, that's roughly what Eddie told us, wasn't it?'

'It must be here somewhere,' Tim muttered. 'C'mon, let's get looking, we can't afford to waste too much time. If we end up coming last, we'll never hear the last of it in the dorm.'

'Yeah, it was bad enough last night having to listen to all their stupid comments,' Andrew grunted. 'And I still can't find where Dean hid my Easter Egg box.'

Tim sighed. 'Not much good at finding things, are you, my old mate?'

5 Comings and Goings

'Look, up there, on that tree!' Andrew cried. 'At last, another one.'

He was beginning to think that the orienteering course was some kind of cruel joke. After giving up the search for that first marker flag, he and Tim had managed to find four of them, but the next two also seemed to be missing. It was all very frustrating.

'Well spotted,' Tim said in relief. 'Right, you go and see what the number is while I check the compass.'

By the time Andrew reported back, Tim had already worked out a possible course to follow. 'Bearing's about sixty degrees, I reckon,' he said, pointing to a distant landmark. 'Let's head for that funny-shaped tree.'

'Which one?'

'The ugly one that looks like Dean appealing for a goal,' Tim laughed. 'See the way its branches spread out?'

Andrew chuckled. 'Wonder how

Dean and Scott are getting on? Better than us, I expect.'

'Everybody will be better than us at this rate!'

But they were not the only pair to be having little success in this part of the woods. Dean had been busy. He was taking great delight in removing some of the flags as soon as Scott had logged their numbers.

'We're gonna have the best score, easy,' he gloated, glancing at his map. 'C'mon, don't bother fiddling around with that compass. Trust me, I know the quickest route to take.'

Scott trudged reluctantly in his partner's wake among the thick undergrowth. He reckoned Dean was in fact going off in the wrong direction for once, but lacked the confidence in his own judgement to say so.

After a few minutes, they found their

way blocked by a deep gully. A fast-flowing stream rippled through it below where they stood, hesitating. 'This shouldn't be here,' Dean muttered. 'Not according to the map. They must have got it wrong somehow.'

'It's not them, it's you!' Scott snarled. 'Admit it, you've gone and got us lost.'

Dean shrugged. 'Well, not lost exactly. Just not quite where I thought we were, that's all. Probably veered off too far to the south of that last track we were on.'

'We'll have to go back and try to find a way round this.'

'Rubbish!' Dean scoffed. 'That'll take too long. We can jump across it here.'

Scott peered doubtfully at the gap. 'It's a bit wide,' he gulped.

'Chicken!' Dean taunted him. 'I'll show you how. Watch!'

He threw his map and compass over the gully, took several steps back and then ran headlong towards it. Dean launched himself through the air to land in a heap on the far side. He stood up, brushed himself down and grinned at his partner.

'See, no bother. Your turn.'

'I thought I heard something crack,' said Scott.

'Yeah, the compass. Went and landed on it!' Dean laughed. 'C'mon, hurry up, chuck your things across. This will make a great short cut.'

Scott swallowed hard, knowing that there was no backing out now. He did as instructed, gathered himself and took a flying leap. Unluckily, his take-off foot slipped and he failed to get the height and distance needed. He dropped short, almost scrambled up

over the edge, but toppled backwards before Dean could grab hold of him.

There was another cracking noise, only this time it wasn't a compass. Scott let out a shriek of pain and crumpled up at the bottom of the gully, partly in the water, as Dean attempted to scramble down to him.

'Think I've bust my arm,' Scott howled. 'I need some help.'

'I'll pull you up.'

'Don't touch me. Just get blowing that whistle.'

'We'll be a laughing stock, having to be rescued,' Dean moaned.

'I don't care,' cried Scott and had to grit his teeth with the pain from his arm. 'Just do it, will you!'

Andrew and Tim heard the distress signal and deserted their own course immediately to respond to the summons. 'Can't be too far away from us,' Tim gasped, hacking through some tangled brambles.

'There's a stream marked on the map over there,' panted Andrew. 'And a long ditch or something. Watch how you go.'

The last person they expected to see was Dean.

'Huh!' he greeted them gruffly. 'Might have known you two would get here first. Come to mock, have you?'

'Don't be stupid,' Andrew retorted. 'What's the matter?'

Dean nodded towards the gully. 'Scott's down there. Idiot went and fell in.'

Tim knelt on the edge. 'Are you all right?'

'What do *you* think?' Scott groaned. 'I'm not trying to play hide-and-seek, you know!'

Two other pairs of boys turned up at that moment, closely followed by Eddie. 'Leave this to me, lads!' the coach ordered, quickly assessing the situation and calling for an ambulance on his mobile phone. 'Start to make your way back to the buses in the clearing. Race is over.'

Dean began to shamble away. 'Not you, young man!' Eddie snapped. 'There's no reason why anybody should be at this spot. No markers round here. You just explain to me how all this happened . . .'

There were two empty beds in the dormitory that night. When Scott's father arrived to take his son home, he was asked to take Dean back with him too.

All that was left as evidence of their occupation were rumpled sheets and a crushed Easter Egg box lying on the top bunk.

'Dean's idea of a farewell present, I guess,' muttered Andrew.

'Good riddance, I say,' Tim replied. 'Feel a bit sorry for Scott, though. He might not have been too bad, really, if Dean hadn't egged him on all the time.'

Andrew pulled a face. 'Not perhaps the best choice of word, that!' he said sadly, dropping the remains of his egg box into the bin.

The following morning, halfway through the final training session, they had a visitor.

'Where's Dean? I thought he was supposed to be here as well. Can't see him anywhere.'

Andrew grinned at his younger brother. 'Good reason for that. He was sent home in disgrace last night.'

'Sent home!' repeated Chris, all agog. 'What did he do?'

'Pinched my Easter Egg for one thing. And some flags.'

'It's a long story,' Tim put in. 'We'll tell you on the way home later. Where's your grandad?'

'Still at the car. I came straight across here when I saw you lot lazing about.'

'Lazing about!' snorted Andrew. 'They're slave-drivers, these coaches! We're just taking a rest while they sort out a few things.'

Tim gave his friend a nervous smile. 'Probably deciding who will be invited back in the summer holidays for another course.'

'Are you both in with a chance, do you reckon?' asked Chris, hoping not to sound as envious as he felt.

'So, so,' shrugged Andrew. 'Especially if Jeff Robson's put in a good word for me.'

'Jeff Robson!' gasped Chris. 'Have you actually met him?'

'Yeah, good mate of mine,' said Andrew, acting cool. 'We've had a few games together this week.'

'Come off it! Who are you trying to kid?'

'Good luck, Andy!' came a cheery voice from behind them as a track-suited figure jogged by and waved. 'See you again.'

'Cheers, Jeff!' shouted Andrew, risking a show of bravado for Chris's benefit. 'Hope your knee's OK soon.'

Chris was speechless.

6 A Born Goalie

'Got any food in that bag of yours?' asked Tim. 'I'm starving.'

Chris shook his head. 'No, only my kit.'

'Your kit!' scoffed Andrew. 'What have you brought that for?'

'Oh, just in case. You never know your luck.'

'Your luck might be in,' Tim smiled. 'Thanks to Dean, we're a goalie short for our eleven-a-side practice match this afternoon.'

'Don't go raising his hopes,' Andrew

said, frowning at Tim. 'We've still got enough people for the game.'

'Just 'cos you don't want your brother joining in the fun.'

'Not that at all,' said Andrew quickly, grateful to hear Eddie whistle the players back into the grids.

Andrew rushed off just as Grandad arrived to watch the activities, but Chris noticed Tim having a word with one of the coaches. His heart leapt when the man looked towards him and began to head in their direction.

'Hi, Chris Weston, is it? I gather you're Andrew's kid brother.'

Chris nodded breathlessly. 'This is our grandad.'

The two men shook hands. 'I'm Kev, United's youth team coach.'

'I remember you as a player,' Grandad

smiled. 'Kevin Barber, United's goal-keeper a while back.'

Kev grinned. 'A long while back! You must have a good memory. Hear your grandson's a keeper as well.'

'Aye, he is, that,' answered Grandad proudly. 'Captain of the school team, too, even though he's the youngest in the side.'

'I wouldn't mind taking a look at what you can do, then, Chris,' Kev said. 'Want to have a go? We could lend you some gear.'

'No need,' Chris said, unzipping his bag and pulling out his goalie gloves. 'I can be ready in two minutes!'

The coach laughed and wandered away as Chris started to change into his kit. 'Told you it might be worth coming prepared,' Grandad said. 'This could be your big break, m'boy. You grab it now with both hands.'

Kev slipped Chris into one of the groups and kept a keen eye on him for the rest of the morning, especially when he had a turn in goal. The coach liked what he saw. Chris and Grandad were both invited to join the party for lunch at United's famous stadium.

The boys who had played in the New Year tournament had been there before, but jumped at the chance to have another look behind the scenes.

Andrew nudged Chris playfully with his elbow as they entered the home dressing room and gazed again at the huge, sunken bath.

'Pity Dean's not around any more,' Andrew said with a wink. 'Remember what happened last time we were in here?'

Chris giggled. 'You promised to drown him!'

'Ah, well,' his brother sighed. 'Another time, maybe. It'll keep.'

The brothers soon had more serious business on their minds back at the training ground, hoping to impress the coaches in the final trial match.

'We're not bothered about the score,' Eddie told the boys as they adjusted their blue and red bibs. 'It's about how each of you plays, not who wins or loses. We'll be swapping people around quite a bit, anyway.'

Andrew was surprised to find himself acting as the Reds' main striker at first, attacking Chris's goal. They grinned at each other as the Reds forced an early corner and when the ball was whipped across the penalty area, fate decided that it would land smack onto Andrew's head. He met it full on the forehead and the ball rocketed towards its target.

It looked a certain goal until Chris flung himself across to his right and palmed the ball wide of the post. The spectacular save earned the new keeper the praise of his teammates and the applause of the two coaches, not to mention Grandad's loud contribution from the touchline.

Chris leapt to claim the second corner, clutching the ball cleanly out of the air. He hugged it safely to his chest

before a long accurate throw out to the winger sent the Blues away on their first attack.

Andrew stood for a moment, hands on hips, shaking his head. 'Still can't believe I didn't score,' he said. 'Well saved, little brother.'

Chris grinned. 'Thanks, I owe you that one. Got me off to a great start.'

Tim was not so helpful. Ten minutes into the game, he ran into a good goal-scoring position, took the ball in his stride and tucked his shot past Chris's left hand as the keeper advanced to narrow the shooting angle.

'Sorry, Chris, had to do it,' Tim apologized, collecting the ball himself from the net. 'Couldn't afford to miss that one.'

Chris smiled ruefully. 'Don't worry, I'll stop your next one instead.'

He did, too, holding on to a rasping

drive from Tim just before one of the many breaks in play for coaching points to be made. By that time, Andrew was already playing in defence for the Blues, and the next period began with all three of them on the same side. They linked up together to create a wonderful goal.

Chris turned defence into attack with a quick throw to his brother and Andrew strode forward over the halfway line. He slid the ball out to Tim and continued his run as Tim's skilful dribbling down the left wing took him past two tackles. Tim had time to measure his cross and planted it perfectly onto Andrew's head at the far post. Goal!

Grandad found Kev standing next to him near the end of the game. 'Like the look of your two grandsons,' he said. 'Andy's had an excellent week

and young Chris has done well today. He's a natural born goalie!'

'Chip off the old block,' Grandad chuckled. 'It was my position too!'

The coaches may not have been keeping count of the score, but both the goalies were. Chris knew he had only let in two goals, compared to the other lad's four, but he almost conceded a third in the very last minute. In a frantic scramble, Chris managed to parry one shot, another hit a post and when the ball was knocked past him again, Andrew was guarding the goal-line and hoofed it away to safety.

The after-match showers were a happy, noisy scene of celebrations and farewells. Most of the players would be seeing each other again soon, though, having already been offered places on

United's summer coaching course – Tim and Andrew included. Kev was even thinking of giving Scott another chance.

Chris was hopeful of being there too. 'We'll be in touch,' Kev had promised him with a wink. 'Keep a watch out for the postman!'

The brothers shared the same towel, Chris having to put up with a wet one after Andrew had grabbed it first. Tim grinned at them. 'Funny it was old Dean who gave Chris his lucky *break*,' he said, stressing the final word. 'He'd be dead mad, if he knew.'

'You still haven't told me what happened,' said Chris.

'No time for that now,' Andrew insisted. 'C'mon, get dressed, slow-coaches. We've got places to go!'

'Like back to the hostel to pick up our cases?' Tim teased him.

'You know what I mean. *Real* places. This could be the start of something BIG!'

THE END

ABOUT THE AUTHOR

Rob Childs was born and grew up in Derby. His childhood ambition was to become an England cricketer or footballer – preferably both! After university, however, he went into teaching and taught in primary and high schools in Leicestershire, where he now lives. Always interested in school sports, he coached school teams and clubs across a range of sports, and ran area representative teams in football, cricket and athletics.

Recognizing a need for sports fiction for young readers, he decided to have a go at writing such stories himself and now has more than thirty books to his name, including the popular *The Big Match* series, published by Young Corgi Books.

Rob now combines his writing career with work helping dyslexic students (both adults and children) to overcome their literacy difficulties. Married to Joy, also a writer, Rob has a "lassie" dog called Laddie and is also a keen photographer.

All Transworld titles are available by post from:

Book Service by Post, PO Box 29,
Douglas, Isle of Man, IM99 1BQ

Credit cards accepted.
Please telephone 01624 675137,
fax 01634 670923
or Internet http://www.bookpost.co.uk or e-mail:
bookshop@enterprise.net for details

Free postage and packing in the UK.
Overseas customers: allow £1 per book (paperbacks)
and £3 per book (hardbacks).